FURIOUS GEORGE GOES BANANAS

A PRIMATE PARODY

MICHAEL REX

G. P. Putnam's Sons 🍌 An Imprint of Penguin Group (USA) Inc.

To Tim,
who has absolutely no concept of
what the word "no" means.

G. P. PUTNAM'S SONS · A division of Penguin Young Readers Group. Published by The Penguin Group.
Penguin Group (USA) Inc., 375 Hudson Street, New York, NY 10014, U.S.A.
Penguin Group (Canada), 90 Eglinton Avenue East, Suite 700, Toronto, Ontario M4P 2Y3, Canada (a division of Pearson Penguin Canada Inc.).
Penguin Books Ltd, 80 Strand, London WC2R ORL, England.
Penguin Ireland, 25 St. Stephen's Green, Dublin 2, Ireland (a division of Penguin Books Ltd.).
Penguin Group (Australia), 250 Camberwell Road, Camberwell, Victoria 3124, Australia (a division of Pearson Australia Group Pty Ltd).
Penguin Books India Pvt Ltd, 11 Community Centre, Panchsheel Park, New Delhi - 110 017, India.
Penguin Group (NZ), 67 Apollo Drive, Rosedale, North Shore 0632, New Zealand (a division of Pearson New Zealand Ltd).
Penguin Books (South Africa) (Pty) Ltd, 24 Sturdee Avenue, Rosebank, Johannesburg 2196, South Africa.
Penguin Books Ltd, Registered Offices: 80 Strand, London WC2R ORL, England.

Published simultaneously in Canada. Manufactured in China by South China Printing Co. Ltd.
Design by Marikka Tamura. Text set in Fink Heavy.
The artist used pencil drawings colored in Photoshop to create the illustrations for this book.

Library of Congress Cataloging-in-Publication Data
Rex, Michael. Furious George goes bananas / Michael Rex. p. cm.
Summary: In this retelling of H. A. and Margret Rey's "Curious George," an ape tries
to return to the jungle after being exploited by a man in a funny hat.
[1. Apes–Fiction. 2. Animals–Treatment–Fiction.] I. Rey, H. A. (Hans Augusto), 1898-1977.
Curious George. II. Rey, Margret. Curious George. III. Title.
PZ7.R32875Fu 2010 [E]–dc22 2009027520
ISBN 978-0-399-25433-8
10 9 8 7 6 5 4 3 2 1

George was a great big ape. He lived in a beautiful jungle.

One day a man in a funny hat saw George and said, "Ooh. What a big monkey. I want him."

The man made a pile of bananas.

When George went to eat the bananas, the man threw a sack over him.

"I got you!" said the man.

The man tried to lift George, but George was too heavy. So the man cut holes in the sack and took George out of the jungle.

They went to the zoo.

"Hello," said the man in the funny hat to the zookeeper.

"Would you like to buy my monkey?"

"Well," said the zookeeper, "he's actually an ape.
Monkeys have tails. But yes, I'll buy him."

So he paid the man lots of money and put George
in a little cage. The floor was hard and cold.
George couldn't run or climb. He couldn't even move.
George hated being locked up!

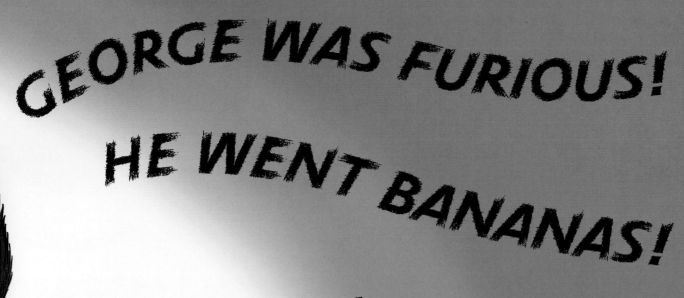

George tied balloons to the zookeeper and
sent him sailing into the sky. Then he ran off.

The man in the funny hat found George. He gave him a pile of bananas. Then he brought George to a construction site.

"My monkey would like a job. Would you like him to work for you?" asked the man in the funny hat.

"Sure," said the foreman. "But he ain't a monkey, he's an ape. A monkey got a tail."

So the foreman paid the man, and George got to work. George carried heavy loads up to the men. It was a hard job, and it was very hot out. George got tired and thirsty, but the foreman wouldn't let him stop.

Then some bricks fell on his head. George hated when bricks fell on his head!

GEORGE WAS FURIOUS!
HE WENT APE!

He smashed the bricks and dropped the foreman in a barrel.
Then he ran off.

The man in the funny hat found George and gave him more bananas and some cold water. Then he brought George to Broadway.

"How would you like to put my monkey in a show?" he asked the director.

"Sounds boffo!" said the director. "But he's an ape, kid. Monkeys have tails, even on Broadway."

"You don't say," said the man in the funny hat as he ran off with his bags of money.

The director gave George lots of bananas and made him do all sorts of silly things on stage. He rode a cow, crashed a bike, and wore goofy pajamas.

The audience laughed and laughed at him.
George hated being laughed at!

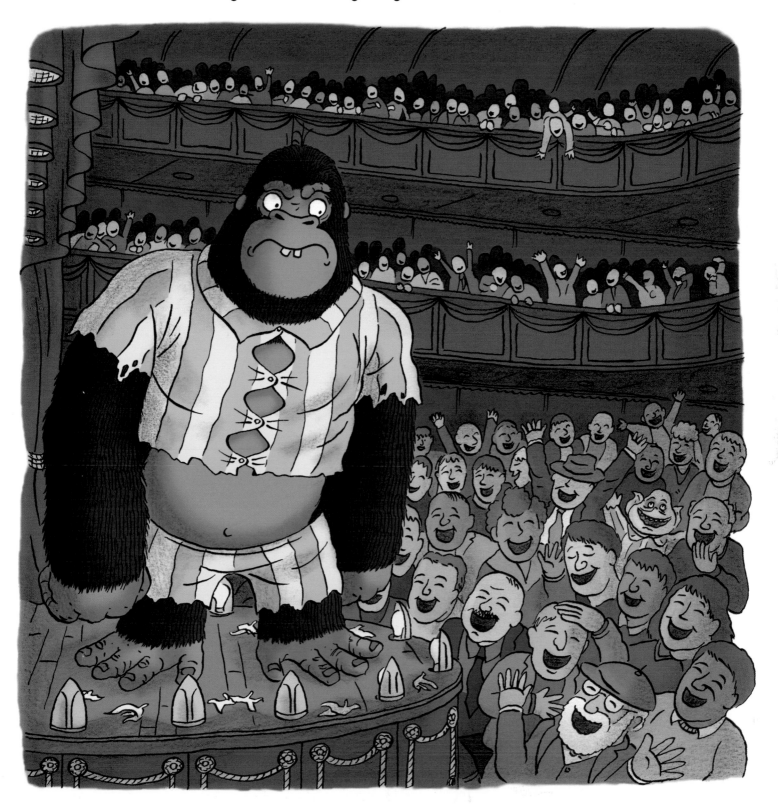

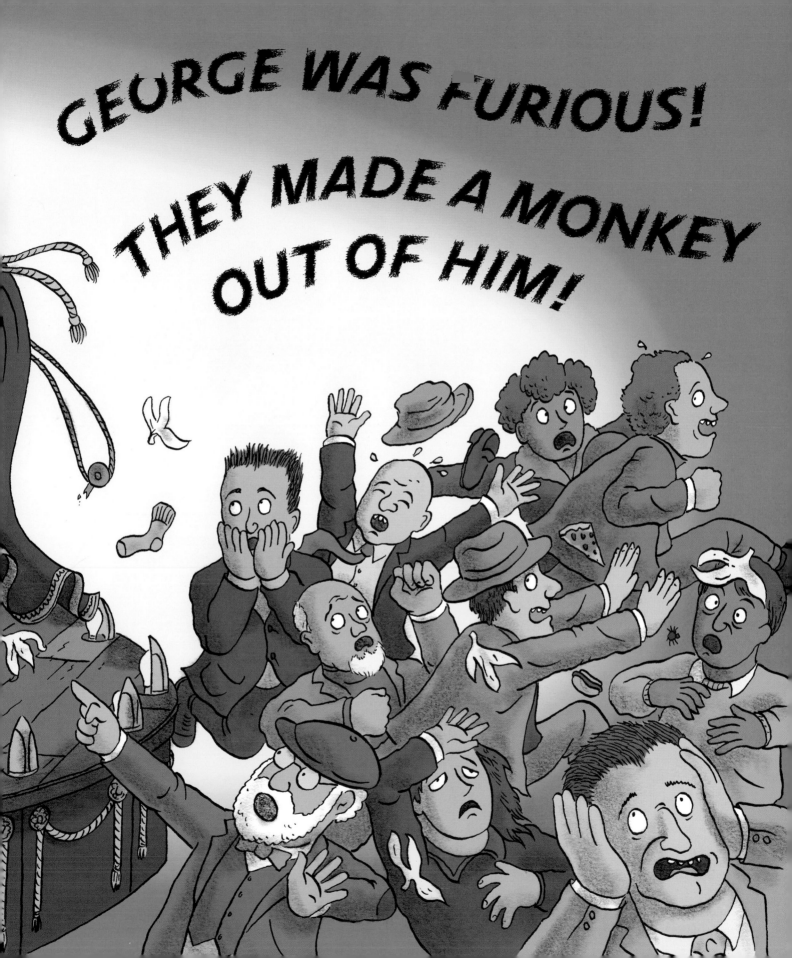

George threw his banana peels everywhere. When the people tried to run away, they all slipped. George didn't mean for them to fall. He just wanted them to stop laughing.

George ran away and hid. The man in the funny hat found him and gave him more bananas. Then he took George to a scientist.

"I heard that you're looking for a monkey to send into outer space. How about using George?"

"Yes. He'll do," said the scientist. "But it is common knowledge that monkeys have tails. George is an ape."

"Yeah, yeah. Ape, shmape," said the man in the funny hat as he counted his pile of money.

The scientist put George in
a space suit. The rocket was ready.
George had to do something!
   He did not want to go into
outer space. He wanted to go home
to the jungle. That rotten man in
the funny hat was the one who
should be going into outer space!

George grabbed the pile of money from the man in the funny hat. He tossed it into the rocket.

The man chased after the money, and
George slammed the hatch behind him.

As the rocket
began to launch,
George jumped on!

The rocket blasted
into the sky.

The man in the funny hat banged on the window. He didn't want to go into outer space either. George leapt off and opened his parachute!

George slowly drifted
back down to earth.

He landed safely in his home,
in the beautiful jungle.